Nothing but trouble

2

For Gita

First published in Great Britain in 1997 by Andersen Press Ltd., 20 Vauxhall Bridge Road, London SW1V 2SA.This paperback edition published in 1998 by Andersen Press Ltd. Published in Australia by Random House Australia Pty., 20 Alfred Street, Milsons Point, Sydney, NSW 2061. All rights reserved. Colour separated in Italy by Fotoriproduzione Grafiche, Verona. Printed and bound in Italy by Grafiche AZ, Verona.

10 9 8 7 6 5 4 3 2

British Library Cataloguing in Publication Data available.

ISBN 0 86264 841 6

This book has been printed on acid-free paper

Nothing but trouble

GUS CLARKE

Andersen Press · London

It had been a bad day for Maisie.

It had started badly.

And it didn't really get any better. Breakfast was a bit of a rush.

And things didn't go well in the bathroom.

Then there'd been the problem with the pigeon on the way to school. Some people say it's lucky. But after that, for Maisie there was nothing but trouble.

First, there was all that time she'd wasted looking for her pencil.

Then for painting she'd had to sit next to Dean.

At playtime she'd been shouted at, right in the middle of a game of marbles.

And P.E. was painful, thanks to Dean.

Lunch was just awful.

She thought her luck had changed when she was chosen to play Sleeping Beauty in the class play.

But guess who played the prince.

Music had given her a bit of a headache. She was very glad when it was time to go home.

Still, she'd made a new friend on the way back from school.

Maisie had been looking forward to tea time, but when it arrived she wasn't really very hungry.

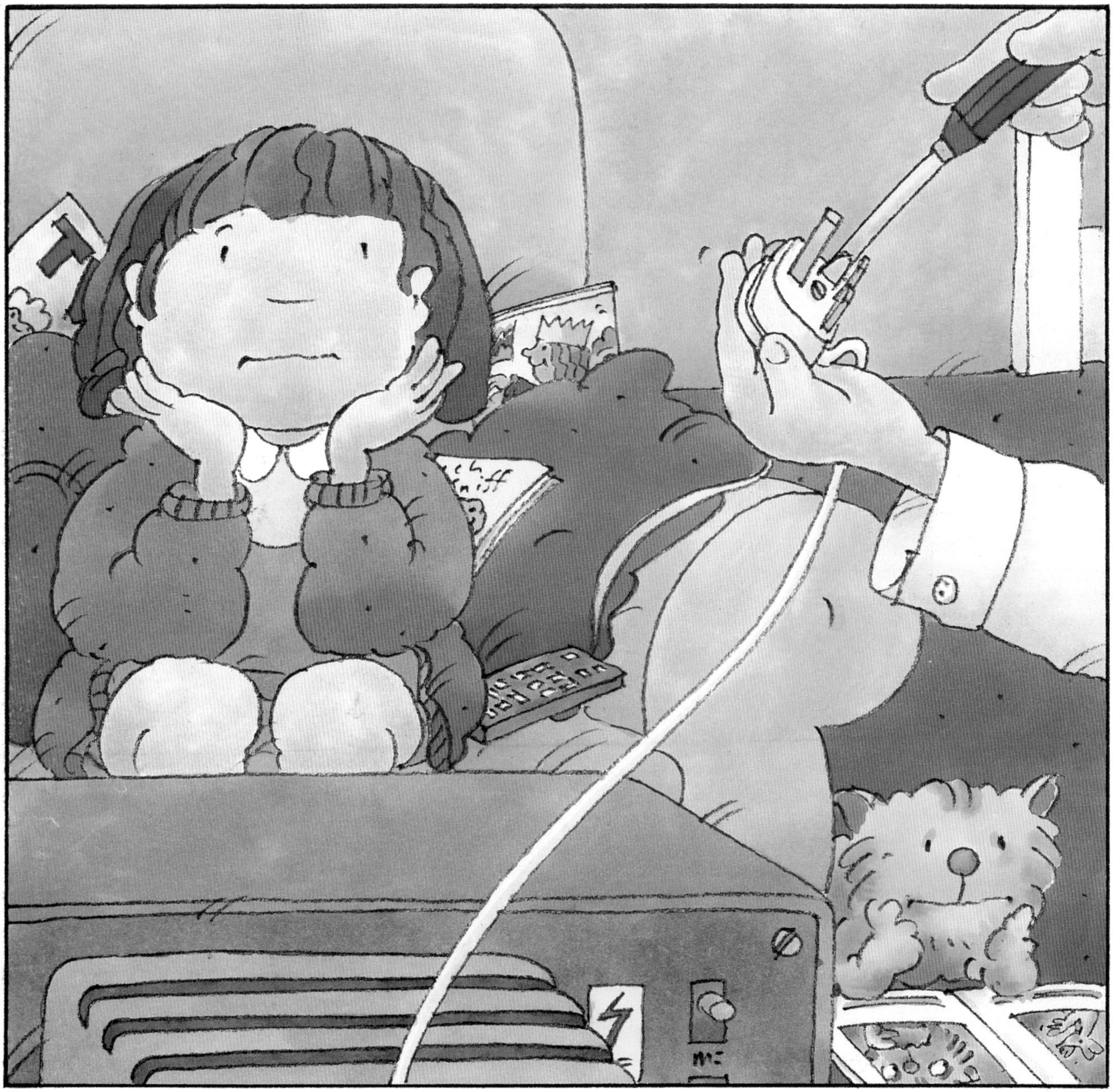

And there was nothing at all on TV.

"Poor Maisie," said Mum. "What a day you've had. Never mind. We'll look forward to a better day tomorrow."

And was it?

Well, it was certainly a much better start.

And breakfast was no trouble at all.

Yes, thought Maisie, it was going very well…

…so far.

More Andersen Press paperback picture books!

OUR PUPPY'S HOLIDAY
by Ruth Brown

SCRATCH 'N' SNIFF
by Gus Clarke

FRIGHTENED FRED
by Peta Coplans

I HATE MY TEDDY BEAR
by David McKee

THE HILL AND THE ROCK
by David McKee

MR UNDERBED
by Chris Riddell

WHAT DO YOU WANT TO BE, BRIAN?
by Jeanne Willis and Mary Rees

MICHAEL
by Tony Bradman and Tony Ross

THE LONG BLUE BLAZER
by Jeanne Willis and Susan Varley

FROG IS A HERO
by Max Velthuijs